D1422474

ISBN 0-86163-494-2 (cased)
ISBN 0-86163-824-7 (limp)

First published 1991 (cased edition)
First published 1996 (limp edition)

Published by Award Publications Limited,
1st Floor, 27 Longford Street,
London, NW1 3DZ

Printed in Belgium

LITTLE RED RIDING HOOD

To Freya

Illustrated by
RENE CLOKE

AWARD PUBLICATIONS

"I want you to take this basket of cakes and fruit to Grandmother," said little Red Riding Hood's mother. "Go straight to the cottage and do not wander off the path through the woods."

Red Riding Hood put on her cloak with the hood.

"I will carry it very carefully," she said. "How lovely the cakes look and Grandmother will enjoy the fruit."

Little Red Riding Hood's father was a wood-cutter so she knew the way through the forest.

She waved goodbye to her mother and skipped away through the village until she came to the path through the woods.

Rabbits scampered amongst the grass and a squirrel looked down at her from a tree; she would like to have played with them but she remembered that she had been told to keep to the path.

But, when she saw some bluebells growing amongst the trees, she longed to pick a bunch. "I won't go far," she said, "I must pick just a few of them for Grandmother."

She knelt down and started gathering some of the flowers.

But the best ones were further away and little Red Riding Hood picked up her basket and wandered through the trees until she had a big armful of bluebells.

Red Riding Hood was so busy picking
the flowers that she did not see a wolf
creeping towards her and was surprised
when she heard a strange voice say,
"Good morning, little girl." She was
frightened for a moment but the wolf
looked very kind so she answered him,
"Good morning, sir."

"What a beautiful bunch of flowers," said the wolf. "Are you picking them for your mother?"

"They are for my grandmother," Red Riding Hood told him.

"She lives all
alone in the
cottage at the
end of the wood
and I am taking her
some cakes and fruit."

"You are a very kind little
girl," said the wolf.
I would like to walk through
the wood with you but
"I am in a hurry and
must say goodbye."
He waved a paw and
trotted off through
the trees.

It took little Red Riding Hood quite a long time to find her way back to the path and the wolf was out of sight before she remembered the way, so she did not see that he had scampered off in the direction of her grandmother's cottage.

When the wolf arrived at the cottage he
crept up the path and knocked at the door.
"Your grandchild is here," he whispered
as gently as he could.

"Pull the bobbin and the latch will go up," answered the grandmother.

The wolf lifted the latch and rushed into the cottage and, before Red Riding Hood's grandmother could call for help, he had gobbled her up!

The wolf looked around the room and saw a night-cap and shawl on a chair.

"Just what I want!" he cried, and looking in a mirror, he put them on.

"Now the little girl will mistake me
for her grandmother," he chuckled and
crept into the big bed.

Little Red Riding Hood walked quickly through the wood until she came to her grandmother's cottage.

She tapped at the door.

"Pull the bobbin and the latch will go up," said the wolf, trying to sound like an old woman.

Picking up her basket and her bunch of flowers, little Red Riding Hood stepped inside.

The room was rather dark but
little Red Riding Hood could
see that someone was in the bed.

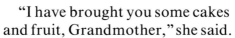

"I have brought you some cakes
and fruit, Grandmother," she said.
"Come nearer, my dear," whispered
the wolf, "I am not feeling very well."

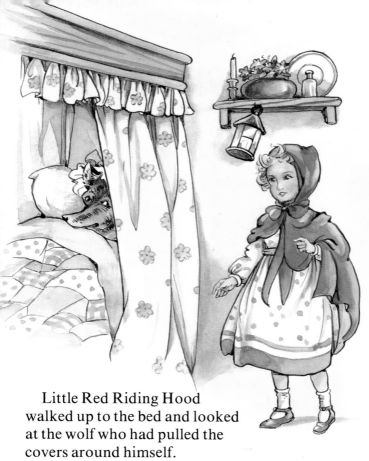

Little Red Riding Hood
walked up to the bed and looked
at the wolf who had pulled the
covers around himself.

"What big ears you have, Grandmother," said
the little girl.

"All the better to hear you with," answered
the wolf.

Red Riding Hood came closer to the
bed for she thought her grandmother
looked rather strange.

"And what big eyes you have,"
she said.

"All the better to see you with,"
the wolf answered.

Then Red Riding
Hood exclaimed,
    "And what big teeth
you have, Grandmother!"

"All the better to
eat you with!" cried
the wolf, and
springing out of bed,
he chased Red Riding Hood round the room.

Red Riding Hood cried out in alarm and
hid behind a chair.
Luckily the wolf tripped over the shawl
he was wearing and the cap fell over his eyes.

The little girl screamed again and her
father, who was cutting wood near by,
heard her cries and dashed into the cottage.
Lifting his axe, he killed the wolf with
one blow.

To their surprise, out stepped the grandmother, for the wolf had swallowed her whole and she was alive and well!

"That skin will make you a nice rug!" laughed the woodcutter.

When Red Riding Hood had given her
grandmother the good things she had
brought in her basket, her father took her
safely home through the forest.

"I won't wander off the path again," she promised her mother when she had told all her adventures, "and I'll never, never talk to a wolf again!"